Anonymous

The Teacher's Journal

Vol. I No. VI

SALZWASSER
VERLAG

Anonymous

The Teacher's Journal

Vol. I No. VI

Reprint of the original, first published in 1859.

1st Edition 2022 | ISBN: 978-3-37513-382-5

Verlag (Publisher): Salzwasser Verlag GmbH, Zeilweg 44, 60439 Frankfurt, Deutschland
Vertretungsberechtigt (Authorized to represent): E. Roepke, Zeilweg 44, 60439 Frankfurt, Deutschland
Druck (Print): Books on Demand GmbH, In de Tarpen 42, 22848 Norderstedt, Deutschland

THE

TEACHER'S

Journal.

Quamdiu quisquam erit, qui audeat te, defendere bibes.

R. W. McAlpine, Editor.

Vol. I. **APRIL, 1859.** **No. VI.**

ALLENTOWN, PENNA.:
R. W. McALPINE, PUBLISHER.
1859.

CONTENTS OF THE APRIL NUMBER.

TEACHER'S JOURNAL.

TERMS—$1 per annum—invariaby in Advance.

ADVERTISING RATES:

IN THE TEACHER'S JOURNAL—FROM AND AFTER MAY 1ST, 1859.

	1 yr.	6 m.	3 m.	1 m.
1 page,	$60.00	$30.00	$20.00	$8.00
½ "	30.00	20.00	12.00	5.00
¼ "	20.00	12.00	8.00	3.00

ADVERTISERS are respectfully requested to state definitely the *space* they wish their advertisements to occupy and the *time* for which they are to be inserted.

Bills will be made out and forwarded as soon as the time for which an adver tisement is entered has expired. No advertisement reckoned less than a quarte page.

OPINIONS OF THE PRESS.

"TEACHER'S JOURNAL.—We have just received the first number of the 'Teacher's Journal published at Allentown, by Messrs. McAlpine & Haines. To say that the Journal is deserv ing a hearty support from the friends of Education, is but paying a poor compliment to th labor and care which characterize its every page. It is interesting and instructive. In it editorials, as well as its selected matter, there is evidence of a mind at work of no mean capa city. We cheerfully recommend the Journal to all who are interested in the cause of edu cation, as a work that should find its way to every fireside. It is calculated to do much goo in the cause to which it is especially devoted, and from what we know of its worthy and ta ented editor, R. W. McAlpine, Esq., if properly sustained, it will prove itself an importar auxiliary in the Educational field."—"Catasauqua Herald."

"THE TEACHER'S JOURNAL, edited by Mr. R. W. McAlpine, of Allentown, Pa., (who also its publisher), is very welcome to our table. We like its matter and its spirit. It evi ces an energy and an ability which inspire a confidence in its success. We fully believe i influence will be felt for good in the cause of Education."—"Educational Herald," N. Y.

TEACHER'S JOURNAL.

Vol. I.　　　　APRIL, 1859.　　　　No. VI.

BOOK BATTLES.

ALTHOUGH text-book makers are generally supposed to be laboring for the public good, it cannot be denied that their labor, such as it is, frequently results in harm. Nor can it be denied that many books are made which should not be used, and that many are consigned to oblivion, which should be in the schools of every town in every state of the Union. The number of new school-books on every subject, published annually, proves one of two things; either that books are made *to sell*, or that conscientious authors discover *something wrong* in every book that is published. It is amusing to watch the war of words between authors or publishers, as to the relative merits of their respective works; and it is none the less amusing to observe the zeal with which disinterested parties enter into a verbal *engagement* to pick each other's favorites to pieces.

The new method of Grammatical Analysis was introduced at about the same time by *Tower, Weld* and *Greene. Tum bellum magnum gesserunt.* There was a dispute about the honor; Weld accusing Greene of using his materials; Greene charging Tower with the larceny of his; and Tower defending himself by honestly declaring that *all* were common thieves from a *Greek grammar* which being imported, was open to all alike.

Our *Websterites* and *Worcesterites* call upon the people to GET THE BEST dictionary. Arithmetic makers praise their own works *of course*—the publishers of A's Geography will not puff B's—and it would be folly to suppose that C, (the author of "The Child's First Steps,") will teach the Alphabet from D's book. Then pedagogues and school-ma'ams, brothers and sisters, while book*makers* disagree, it behooves *us*, the book-*users* to decide. And how *shall* we decide? Shall we take the *ipse dixit* of an extravagant advertising publisher? Shall we place into the hands of our pupils, a new book, because it contains five pages of testimonials from those who have probably never opened it? Shall we rely upon the judgment of an Editor, who perhaps, fears to give his *own* opinion of the book, but prefers to use that of the author?

Allow us to anticipate your honest reply; you will judge for yourselves; you will give to your pupils what you think is best for them to learn and for you to teach—but for yourselves you will provide *all* the old and new works which should compose a Teacher's library, and to which he may be able to turn for reference at a moment's warning. Yes, buy them *all*—at least as many as you can. Many publishers supply Teachers with works for examination, at a very reduced price. *Send* for these works—examine them, take them to your schoolrooms, place them where your pupils can have access to them at all hours of the day, and select the books you wish your classes to use. Do not be guided by the opinions of others in the choice of a book, *unless you are not able to judge for yourselves*, in which case, dismiss your pupils, lock your schoolrooms, hand the keys to your Directors, and *hire out* as a teamster. And—

But we sat down with the intention of writing something concerning "The Battles of the Books."

We may glean from these discussions of the merits of books, many important facts,—and many hints and suggestions which we should take to ourselves and our schoolrooms. We learn that wise men differ among themselves—(*Vide Cæsaris Commentarii, Lib.* 1, *Cap.* 1 for context.)

We learn that although the points of difference between the authors' ideas are not all-important, a vast amount of information which is necessary for a respectable scientific argument, even on a trifling subject, is made common property—that which has been hidden for years, perhaps for ages, within the dusty covers of unopened volumes—is regenerated—rejuvenated, and adds something to our stock of general knowledge. In following the disputants thro' a labyrinth of words and ideas, stopping where they stop, drinking where they drink, we become acquainted with their journey, with the sources whence they derived their strength, with the difficulties they encountered in attempting to live in the dark that which was invisible during the day—and we are thus enabled to satisfy ourselves as to the pleasure and profit of a similar journey. What though the object for which we labor be trivial—unimportant; if in this labor, we learn the names and uses of hundreds of things whose names and uses were before unknown to us? We are called to visit an out-of-the-way town or village in the interior of Russia. Should we neglect the journey because the place and the people to whom we are called, are devoid of interest to us? Think of the thousand novel and pleasing objects we shall pass on our journey—the lofty mountains of which we have read, and of whose shape, size, beauty or grandeur we know nothing—of the winding rivers of the old world, whose names we have learned, parrot-like, from some popular text-book on Geography—of the Homes of the Poets—the abodes of the Philosophers and Statesmen and Kings of ancient times, whose names and deeds are to us like fairy tales, whose reality is like the reality of the dream—of the ruins of lordly towers and kingly palaces, beneath whose domes and within whose walls were enacted those scenes the recital of which has made our very blood curdle.— Think of the valley of the Rhine, the Alps of Switzerland, the public schools of Prussia, the army of Austria, the dykes of Holland—Leyden and Vienna and Berlin and Moscow, and the scores of cities of note, thro' which we may pass—

the manners and customs of the people—the languages and dialects of provinces —the currencies of twenty different principalities and kingdoms! Are not these wayside gleanings a recompense for our labor? Aside from motives of personal satisfaction—what a fund of information—real—solid—substantial information we have, on which others as well as ourselves may draw. We return to our schoolrooms. Are we not better able *now* to instruct and amuse and delight our pupils than we were before?

We learn to overcome old prejudices. He who has changed none of his opinions, has corrected none of his mistakes. We had been taught that this or that people were barbarous. We *know* that they are civilized. We had been taught that a certain system of education tends to degrade and debase a nation—we have learned by living where this system is pursued that the people are noble-hearted, liberal and well informed. Has our Journey been a useless one? Is it not better to know truth than to believe error?

ERRORS CORRECTED.

"The learning the dead languages is necessary to an acquaintance with our own."

The objective case should not follow the participle *preceded by an article.* When the participle follows an article, it loses almost entirely its participial character and becomes more noun-like; a preposition should follow the participle in this example.

"Every individual has their own faults." *Individual* is singular; *every* signifies all taken separately. In idea these sentences are the same;

Every individual has his (own) faults,

Each individual has his (own) faults,

All individuals have their (own) faults.

"He plead (pled) for the life of his brother." (Pleaded.)

"Ghosts of ghastly recollections troop about my bed of nights."—*Thackeray's Ballad of King Canute.* Of nights should be "*a* nights," being a contraction of "*at* nights," and not "*of* nights." A kindred mistake is seen in the common expression "now-*a*-days," which is a translation of the Latin *nunc dierum*, that is, "now-*of*-days." The obscure sound of *o* and *a* as heard in honor or polar, has not always been carefully or uniformly written. *A*-fore-time is a corruption of *of*-fore-time; many-*a*-sheep, of many-*of*-sheep; half-*a*-dollar, of half-*of*-(a) dollar.

If Phonography ever prevails, and recognizes the obscure sound of *o* and *a*, the etymons of many thousand words will be obscured or confounded, and this enevitable result of phonography is the most serious objection that we have seen brought against the proposed reform of the alphabet; but the etymology, though curious and interesting, and highly useful in tracing the origin of nations and races, is less important than the vast saving of time which would be made by having one letter for each simple sound, and one sound for each letter. Dickens and other modern writers frequently use expressions like the following,—I went there *of* a Monday; He loved to go there *of* evenings--and the lovers of light reading are beginning to imitate these blunders, for it is always easier to imitate the defects than the excellencies of the great."—*Mass. Com. Sch. Jour.*, 1851.

"We had just *eat* our supper when he left us." Eat, Ate, (improperly pronounced *et*,) (had) Eaten.

"Father, I can neither *lay* nor *set*." "Then, *go to roost*," says the father.

"A new pair of shoes," should be "a pair of new shoes."

"Seven couple were at the wedding," "Seven *couples*, &c."

"*Are* your hair coarse?" "My hair *are not* coarse, neither *are* my head gray." —(Pennsylvania.)

"*Are these molasses* Sugar-house?" "They *air* stranger."—(Arkansas.)

"Haow kee-*yind* in him to drive the caow from the track. The kyars mought a' killed her."—(Yankee and Virginia.)

"I am going *into* my trunk" (to). You go *into* a house when you *enter* it—you can go *in* the house if you *walk* from one room to another.

"People *seldom ever* like to be censured." Omit *ever*.

"See *if* it rains." (whether.)

"These passages *had better have been buried*." This is an awkward sentence. If the teacher believes in the nonsense of the potential mood, "had have been buried" is a precious example of it. (Were better buried.)

"If you *had have* sent me the first number of the Journal—I would have subscribed to it." (Letter from an indignant correspondent who is indebted to us for the coat he wears.) In what tense is *had have sent?* This is a very common error. In conversation, we hear it uttered frequently as if the two words were one; *hadder*—if you *hadder* sent, &c. Omit the word *have*.

Should in place of *would*—and *for* instead of *to*.

"Please *leave* me speak." (Nineteen out of twenty school-children.) "*Let* me speak" is preferable. *Leave* means to abandon, to relinquish, to desert; *let* signifies to allow, to permit, &c.

"This is made of a mixture of copper and of tin." A mixture consisting of one ingredient can not be made. "A mixture of copper"—is one—(a mixture) of tin is one. Omit the last *of*.

"If it *would* not have been for Arnold &c." If it had not been for Arnold, or, But for Arnold &c.

"One of my books *were* lost." (A pupil.) How many books *were* lost? "One." *One book were* lost? "One of my books *was* lost."

"If it will be a pleasant day to-morrow we shall go." Generally considered incorrect. Why?

"Are you aware that it snows?" Why do we call *are* plural, yet consider *you* singular?

An exchange paper quotes from our last article on "Errors," a rule for the position of the conjunction "and," when two or more of the same kind or class of words are used—but considers us in the wrong. We would have the sentence punctuated thus: virtue, honor and character were lost. Our reasons are plain; should we supply the ellipsis, the sentence would read, virtue and honor and character were lost, in which no comma is necessary. Why? Because the conjunction fills its place. We are inclined to think that our fellow craftsman was taught when he read, to pause at the comma, as if the comma was placed in the sentence to regulate the voice. We are aware that Goold Brown uses the comma after each word of the same kind in the sentence, but we are also aware that neither he nor Wilson nor Mitch nor Craig nor Clark has ever given a reason for so doing.

DIALOGUE BETWEEN A PUBLISHER AND HIS PATRON.

BY WM. B. FOWLE.

"Had not qui and y pence"

PATRON.—You need not urge payment so furiously. You have called on me to pay a dozen times.

PUBLISHER.—Not exactly so, we have called on you a dozen times to pay.

PAT.—Well that is eleven times too many, and you should be ashamed to ask so many times for one poor dollar.

PUB.—We feel ashamed, and nothing but necessity could drive us to it. Yet, if you will not take offence, we would suggest that, if 'tis shame in us to ask payment of such an honest debt, 'tis double shame in him who does not pay; and if 'tis meanness to require the payment of so small a debt, 'tis double meanness not to pay the trifle.

PAT.—You urge the payment as if you suppose I never intend to pay.

PUB.—The best ground for supposing so, lies in the fact that you do not pay. What proof have I that he who obeys not God will ever turn to him?

PAT.—You mix great things with small.

PUB.—No, He hath said by his Apostle, "Owe no man anything;" and he who does incur a debt he never intends to pay, or he who has incurred one honestly, and, being unable to pay, yet offers no excuse, breaks the commandment, and must repent or not expect forgiveness.

PAT.—The world will not to ruin fall if this great debt remains unpaid!

PUB.—My little world may not survive the shock. It is a small affair, but the smallness is on your part, not on mine. If payment you refuse because you owe but one poor dollar, then your neighbor may refuse, and so many thousands do, with as good reason, and each but one dollar save, while I lose thousands. It it far worse to withhold one dollar from the poor than to withhold a thousand from the rich, though this is no excuse, if you can pay.

PAT.—Yet still a dollar seems too trifling for contention such as this.

PUB.—It takes two parties to make a quarrel, and though the cause of the contention be a trifle, I see not why 'tis smaller to one party than to the other. But the amount is less important to yourself than one thing else that has not yet been named.

PAT.—Out with it! Let me know the worst. I have subscribed and do intend to pay. What lack I yet?

PUB.—Subscription implies obligation, promise. You have promised me to pay in advance, and have not paid at all. If 'tis mean in me to payment ask for one poor dollar, when the debt is just, and I have a right to ask, then surely it is meaner far to break one's promise for that same poor dollar.

PAT.—Well, you may erase my name, I do not want your Journal longer.

PUB.—I think you mean you do not wish it, and I interpret thus your thought. You will continue to receive the publication if I will continue to endure the wrong. But if you are required to do but justice, and to keep your promise, you will no longer patronize the work!

PAT.—I have a faint suspicion that I have paid already.

PUB.—I have more than a faint suspicion that you have not paid; and, let me add, that this suspicion would have come with better grace if sooner named. He who endeavors to extenuate a fault that he allows, when he has failed to extenuate, should not deny that any fault has been committed, or claim that reparation has been made already.

PAT.—The shortest way is to pay the dollar, for I hate disputes.

PUB.—I hate them too, especially when I have the worst of the argument. There, sir, is your bill receipted.

PAT.—This is the fifth bill I have received for this small sum.

PUB.—It is the fifth that I have written for the same small sum. The hardship is in writing not in receiving so many.

PAT.—You seem to have the argument at your tongue's end.

PUB.—I have to rehearse it several times a day. I wish I could forget and never need it.

PAT.—Why send the paper till you have the pay?

PUB.—I have the promise, and should give offence to say it was not worth a dollar. But it is fair to inquire why you receive the paper, till you pay; the rule works both ways, surely.

PAT.—You have your profit on the work or you would not publish it.

PUB.—I should little gain did all subscribers pay, but, as it is, I nothing gain, and only work for the good that I may do. (*Receiving the dollar,*) I thank you, sir.

PAT.—It hardly deserves thanks.

PUB.—I do not thank you for the justice done, but for the trouble I am saved. It costs as much thus to collect the debts, as to prepare and publish all the work. Ought I not then to thank you as I do? We publishers shall ne'er be doomed with Sisiphus hereafter to roll heavy stones up hill, and make no progress; but having rolled them up so long, methinks, we shall be rather doomed to roll them down hereafter, on such delinquents as forget us here.

Not a tree,
A plant, a leaf, a blossom, but contains
A folio volume. We may read, and read,
And read again, and still find something new,
Something to please, and something to instruct,
Even in the humble weed.—ANONYMOUS.

PECULIARITIES OF NUMBERS—*Continued.*

BY THE EDITOR.

IF the sum of the squares of two consecutive numbers be divided by the sum of the numbers, the quotient will equal the smaller number and a fraction whose denominator is the sum of the numbers and whose numerator, the larger number.

$$\text{The square of } \quad 9 = 81, \qquad\qquad 11^2 = 121,$$
$$\text{`` \qquad `` \qquad `` } 10 = 100, \qquad\qquad 12^2 = 144,$$
$$\text{Sum of Sq's} = 181, \qquad\qquad \text{Sum of Sq's} = 265,$$
$$\text{Sum of No's} = 19: \qquad\qquad \text{Sum of No's} = 23:$$
$$181 + 19 = 9\tfrac{10}{19} \qquad\qquad 265 \times 23 = 11\tfrac{12}{23}.$$

Here we perceive that we have for the integers the smaller numbers 9 and 11; for numerators, the larger numbers 10 and 12; for denominators, $9 + 10 = 19$, and $11 + 12 = 23$.

Let 24 be the dividend and 3 the divisor; (quotient, 8.) Now take 8 (with a cipher,) as a dividend, and 24 as a divisor, then will the quotient be 3 (as before) with the addition of a fraction whose numerator is 8 and whose denominator is 24.

$$24 \div 3 = 8 \qquad 30 \div 3 = 10 \qquad 51 \div 3 = 17$$
$$80 \div 24 = 3\tfrac{8}{24} \qquad 100 \div 30 = 3\tfrac{10}{30} \qquad 170 \div 51 = 3\tfrac{17}{51}$$

Notice that the fraction in these examples is always $\frac{1}{3}$.

$$26 \div 3 = 8\tfrac{2}{3}: \quad 8\tfrac{2}{3} \times 10 = 86\tfrac{2}{3}. \quad 86\tfrac{2}{3} \div 26 = 3\tfrac{2\,1\,8}{26} = 3\tfrac{1}{3}$$

The product of the squares of two numbers is equivalent to the square of their product.

$$5^2 = 25 \qquad 4 \times 5 = 20 \qquad 400 = 20^2.$$
$$4^2 = 16 \qquad 25 \times 16 = 400$$

The square of a number equals 4 times the square of half the number, 9 times the square of one third of it, 16 times the square of one fourth &c.

$$25^2 = 625,$$
$$125^2 = 625 \times 25. \quad (125 = 5 \times 25.)$$

The square of 14 is 196, what is the square of 24? $14 + 24 = 38.$

196	13^2 is 169	169
38	$33 - 13$ is $(2)0^*$	92
$\overline{576}$ is 24^2	$33 + 13$ is 46	$\overline{1089}$ is 33^2
	$46 \times 2^*$ is 92	

To find the square of any number between 25 and 50: Take the difference between 25 and the given number, subtract this difference* from 25, square the remainder and add the difference* to the left hand figure of the square.

Required the square of 38. $38 - 25$ is 13^*; $25 - 13$ is 12; 12^2 is 144.

$$\begin{array}{r} 144 \\ 13^* \\ \hline 1444 = 38^2 \end{array}$$

No number ending in 2 can be a perfect square; no number ending in 3 can be a perfect square; no number ending in 7 can be a perfect square, &c., &c.

Cubes end in 0, 1, 2, 3, 4, 5, 6, 7, 8 and 9.

THE GRAMMATICAL STUDY OF THE ENGLISH LANGUAGE.

CONCLUDED.

THE difficulty of instructing youth in any thing that pertains to language, lies not so much in the fact that its philosophy is above their comprehension, as in our own ignorance of certain parts of so vast an inquiry;—in the great multiplicity of verbal signs; the frequent contrariety of practice; the inadequacy of memory; the inveteracy of ill habits; and the little interest that is felt when we speak merely of words.

The grammatical study of our language was early and strongly recommended by Locke and other writers on education, whose character gave additional weight to an opinion which they enforced by the clearest arguments. But either for want of a good grammar, or for lack of teachers skilled in the subject and sensible of its importance, the general neglect so long complained of as a grievous imperfection in our methods of education, has been but recently and partially obviated. "The attainment of a correct and elegant style," says Dr. Blair, "is an object which demands application and labor. If any imagine they can catch it merely by the ear, or acquire it by the slight perusal of some of our good authors, they will find themselves much disappointed. The many errors, even in point of grammar, the many offences against purity of language, which are committed by writers who are far from being contemptible, demonstrate, that a careful study of the language is previously requisite, in all who aim at writing it properly."

"To think justly, to write well, to speak agreeably, are the three great ends of academic instruction. The Universities will excuse me, if I observe, that both are, in one respect or other, defective in these three capital points of education. While in Cambridge the general application is turned altogether on speculative knowledge, with little regard to polite letters, taste, or style; in Oxford the whole attention is directed towards classical correctness, without any sound foundation laid in severe reasoning and philosophy. In Cambridge and in Oxford, the art of speaking agreeably is so far from being taught, that it is hardly talked or thought of. These defects naturally produce dry unaffecting compositions in the one; superficial taste and puerile elegance in the other; ungracious or affected speech in both."

"A grammatical study of our own language makes no part of the ordinary method of instruction, which we pass through in our childhood; and it is very seldom we apply ourselves to it afterward. Yet the want of it will not be effectually supplied by any other advantages whatsoever. Much practice in the polite world, and a general acquaintance with the best authors, are good helps; but alone [they] will hardly be sufficient: We have writers, who have enjoyed these advantages in their full extent, and yet cannot be recommended as models of an accurate style. Much less then will, what is commonly called learning, serve the purpose; that is, a critical knowledge of ancient languages, and much reading of ancient authors: The greatest critic and most able grammarian of the last age, when he came to apply his learning and criticism to an English author, was frequently at a loss in matters of ordinary use and common construction in his own vernacular idiom."

"To the pupils of our public schools the acquisition of their own language, whenever it is undertaken, is an easy task. For he who is acquainted with several grammars already, finds no difficulty in adding one more to the number. And this, no doubt, is one of the reasons why English engages so small a proportion of their time and attention. It is not frequently read, and is still less frequently written. Its supposed facility, however, or some other cause, seems to have drawn upon it such a degree of neglect as certainly cannot be praised. The students in those schools are often distinguished by their compositions in the learned languages, before they can speak or write their own with correctness, elegance, or fluency. A classical scholar too often has his English style to form, when he should communicate his acquisitions to the world. In some instances it is never formed with success; and the defects of his expression either deter him from appearing before the public at all, or at least counteract in a great degree the influence of his work, and bring ridicule upon the author. Surely these evils might easily be prevented or diminished."

"It is also said that those who know Latin and Greek, generally express themselves with more clearness than those who do not receive a liberal education. It is indeed natural that those who cultivate their mental powers, write with more clearness than the uncultivated individual. The mental cultivation, however, may take place in the mother tongue as well as in Latin or Greek. Yet the spirit of the ancient languages, farther is declared to be superior to that of the modern. I allow this to be the case; but I do not find that the English style is improved by learning Greek. It is known that literal translations are miserably bad, and yet young scholars are taught to translate, word for word, faithful to their dictionaries. Hence those who do not make a peculiar study of their own language, will not improve in it by learning, in this manner, Greek and Latin. Is it not a pity to hear, what I have been told by the managers of one of the grst institutions of Ireland, that it was easier to fine ten teachers for Latin and Greek, than one for the English language, though they proposed double the salary to the latter? Who can assure us that the Greek orators acquired their superiority by their acquaintance with foreign languages; or, is it not obvious, on the other hand, that they learned ideas and expressed them in their mother tongue?"

"Dictionaries were compiled, which comprised all the words, together with their several definitions, or the sense each one expresses and conveys to the mind. These words were analyzed and classed according to their essence, attributes, and functions. Grammar was made a rudiment leading to the principles of all thoughts, and teaching by simple examples, the general classification of words and their subdivisions in expressing the various conceptions of the mind. Grammar is then the key to the perfect understanding of languages; without which we are left to wander all our lives in an intricate labyrinth, without being able to trace back again any part of our way." Again: "Had it not been for his dictionary and his grammar, which taught him the essence of all languages, and the natural subdivision of their component parts, he might have spent a life as long as Methuselah's, in learning words, without being able to attain to a degree of perfection in any of the languages." "Indeed, it is not easy to say, to what degree, and in how many different ways, both memory and judgement may be improved by an intimate acquaintance with grammar; which is therefore, with good reason, made the first and fundamental part of literary education. The greatest orators, the most elegant scholars, and the most accomplished men of business, that have appeared in the world, of whom I need only mention Cæsar and Cicero, were not only studious of grammar, but most learned grammarians."

Here, as in many other parts of my work, I have chosen to be liberal of quotations; not to show my reading, or to save the labor of composition, but to give the reader the satisfaction of some other authority than my own. In commending the study of English grammar, I do not mean to discountenance that degree of attention which in this country is paid to other languages; but merely to use my feeble influence to carry forward a work of improvement, which, in my opinion, has been wisely begun, but not sufficiently sustained. In consequence of this improvement, the study of grammar, which was once prosecuted chiefly through the medium of the dead languages, and was regarded as the proper business of those only who were to be instructed in Latin and Greek, is now thought to be an appropriate exercise for children in elementary schools. And the sentiment is now generally admitted, that even those who are afterwards to learn other languages, may best acquire a knowledge of the common principles of speech from the grammar of their vernacular tongue. This opinion appears to be confirmed by that experience which is at once the most satisfactory proof of what is feasible, and the only proper test of what is useful.   *Goold Brown.*

HYPOTHESES OF THE ANTEDILUVIAN WORLD, &c.—*Continued.*

DR. HUTTON'S THEORY.

IN the first volume of the Edinburgh Philosophical Transactions, Dr. Hutton has laid down a new theory of the earth, perhaps the most elaborate and comprehensive that has hitherto appeared; to give a general abstract of it would much exceed the bounds allotted to this chapter, Wherefore, all that can be done here is, to point out some of the most striking passages.

He says, the general view of the terrestrial system conveys to our mind a fabric erected in wisdom, and that it was originally formed by design as an habitation for living creatures. In taking a comprehensive view of the mechanism of the globe, we observe three principal parts of which it is composed, and which, by being properly adapted to one another, form it into an habitable world; these are the solid body of the earth, the waters of the ocean, and the atmosphere surrounding the whole. On these Dr. Hutton observes:

1. The parts of the terrestrial globe more immediately exposed to our view, are supported by a central body, commonly supposed, but without any good reason, to be solid and inert.

2. The aqueous part, reduced to a spherical form by gravitation, has become oblate by the earth's centrifugal force. Its use is to receive the rivers, to be a fountain of vapors, and to afford life to innumerable animals, as well as to be the source of growth and circulation to the organized bodies of the earth.

3. The irregular body of land raised above the level of the sea, is by far the most interesting, as immediately necessary to the support of animal life.

4. The atmosphere surrounding the whole is evidently necessarry for innumerable purposes of life and vegetation, neither of which could subsist a moment without it.

Having thus considered the mechanism of the globe, he proceeds to investigate the powers by which it is upheld: these are the gravitating and projectile forces by which the planets are guided; the influence of light and heat, cold and condensation: to which may be added electricity and magnetism.

With regard to the beginning of the world, though Dr. Hutton does not pretend to lay aside the Mosaic accounts respecting the origin of man, yet he endeavors to prove, that the marine animals are of much higher antiquity than the human race.

The solid parts of the globe are, in general, composed of sand, gravel, argillaceous and calcareous strata, or of these mixed with some other substances.

Sand is separated and sized by streams and currents; gravel is formed by the mutual attrition of stones agitated in water; and marly or argillaceous strata have been collected by subsiding in water in which those earthy substances had floated. Thus, so far as the earth is formed of these materials, it would appear to have been the production of water, wind, and tides.

The doctor's next inquiry, is into the origin of our land, which he seems willing to derive entirely from the exuviæ of marine animals! After adducing some arguments in support of this opinion, the principal of which is drawn from the quantity of marine productions found in different parts of the earth, he says, "The general amount of our reasoning is this; that nine-tenths perhaps, or 99 hundredths of this earth, so far as we see, have been formed by natural operations of the globe, in collecting loose materials, and depositing them at the bottom of the sea, consolidating those collections in various degrees, and either elevating these consolidated masses above the level on which they were formed, oo lowering the level of that sea."

With respect to the different strata, he thinks it most probable that they have been consolidated by heat and fusion; and this hypothesis he imagines, will solve every difficulty respecting them; and, as the question is of the greatest importance in natural history, he discusses it to a considerable length. He considers metals of every species as the vapor of the mineral regions, condensed occasionally in the crevices of the land.

His next consideration is the means by which the different strata have been elevated from the bottom of the ocean; (for he looks upon it as an indubitable fact that the highest points of our land have been for ages at the bottom of the ocean;) and concludes, that the land on which we dwell has been elevated from a lower situation by the same agent which has been employed in consolidating the strata, in giving them stability, and preparing them for the purpose of the living world. This agent is matter, actuated by extreme heat, and expanded with amazing force.

The doctor imagines the world to be eternal, and endued with renovating power; for he says, "When the former land of this globe had been complete, so as to begin to waste and be impaired by the encroachment of the sea, the present land began to appear above the surface of the ocean. In this manner, we suppose a due proportion of land and water to be always preserved upon the surface of the globe, for the purpose of a habitable world, such as we possess." After endeavoring to prove a succession of worlds in the system of nature, he concludes his dissertation in these words; "The result, therefore, of our present inquiry is, that we find no vestige of a beginning, no prospect of an end."

[*From Wm. B. Fowle's Journal*—1851.]

A GEOGRAPHICAL LESSON.—THE SOUTH POLE.

ALTHOUGH no navigator has entered the Arctic Ocean by Davis's Strait and left it at Bhering's, few persons probably doubt that there is a passage, and that, north of America, Europe and Asia, and separated from them, is a large tract of land, a Continent, if you please, of which Greenland is probably a part, and on which is the spot called the North Pole. So, it is satisfactorily shown that, south of America, Africa and New Holland, is another tract, a Southern Continent, which surrounds the point called the South Pole; and, although but little pecuniary profit can be expected from discoveries in this region, it has been visited by many navigators, at much expense and great risk. No one has approached so near the South as some have approached the North Pole, but the Southern or Antarctic Continent has actually been circumnavigated, and there can be no doubt that science and commerce will be greatly benefitted by labors, which, to the superficial observer, may seem to be worse than useless, because expensive and dangerous.

No maps that have been made for schools give any complete drawings of the portions of this Southern Continent ascertained beyond any doubt, but it will not be difficult for any teacher to mark the coast, as we shall describe it, on the outline or other maps of his school, and then it will be a useful exercise to let the pupils copy what is thus drawn and described by the teacher.

Bartholomew Diaz, a Portuguese, excelled all other navigators before his time, when, in 1486, he discovered the Cape of Good Hope, which his countryman, Vasco de Gama, doubled (sailed round) a few years afterwards. In 1501, Vespucci, in the service of Portugal, sailed down the coast of South America to the 52d degree of South Latitude. When he turned back, he is supposed to have been between the Falkland Isles and Patagonia. Magellan, with a Spanish fleet of five small vessels, the largest measuring only 120 tons, discovered the Strait that bears his name, in 1520. The natives wearing very clumsy things for shoes, he called them Patagones, or *clumsy-hoofed*, and seeing many fires on shore during the night, he called the land Terra del Fuego, or *Land of Fire*. While at anchor there, some the natives visited the ships, and the Spaniards, either de-ceived in regard to their stature, or wishing to embellish their narratives, reported them to be giants, and the fable was believed until quite modern times. Magellan was the first who sailed entirely round the globe, and noticed the two facts, that by constantly sailing West, or away from home, he in time arrived at home, and the year which, had he staid at home, would have had 365 days, had only 364. The earth turns from West to East, and, if a person stays still, the sun will rise to his eye once in every 24 hours; but, if he sails westward, it will take the place where he is a little more than 24 hours to turn from sunrise, and this difference will amount to a whole day in one circumnavigation of the globe.

Balboa, a Spaniard, had seen the Pacific from the Isthmus of Darien; Magellan was the first European that entered it with ships. He crossed the Pacific, and was killed on the Philippine Islands by the natives, only one of his vessels returning home.

Sir Francis Drake, in the service of England, passed through the Strait of Magellan, and being driven by storms towards the South, landed on the island of Terra del Fuego, and found the southernmost point of it, which he supposed to be the end of the world. Here he lay down, and, stretching his body as far as he could beyond the point, he boasted that "he had been farther South than any man as yet known." De Weert, a Dutchman, in 1598, discovered the Falkland Isles; and Gerritz, who was in the same fleet, being driven as far South as 64°, discovered islands, which were afterwards re-discovered and called the South Shetlands (lat. 64°, and W. long. 60°). A subsequent Dutch expedition sailed round the Southern extremity of America, and named one island Staten Land (States Land), in honor of the United States of Holland, and the most Southern point of another island was called Cape Horn, in honor of one of their ships which had just been lost. Sailors generally speak of doubling *The Horn*, and they say the island is shaped like a horn, but the name first appears in history as we have mentioned. Le Maire, a merchant of Amsterdam, fitted out this expedition, and gave the command of it to William Schouten and his own son, in 1615. Another Dutch fleet in 1623, under Jacques le Hermite, went as far South as 60°, and rounded Cape Horn without seeing it. Torres, who sailed West from Lima, probably discovered Tahiti, Pitcairn's Island, and Australia, or New Holland. A Dutch ship sent by Van Diemen, the governor of Batavia, under Tasman, doubled the island at the Southern point of Australia, and named it after the Governor. The Dutch Government, in honor of their country, called the great island New Holland. Tasman also discovered New Zealand, and supposed it adjoined Terra del Fuego. Cook, in 1769, visited Australia, and called a portion of it New South Wales. He sailed round New Zealand, and showed that it had no connection with Terra del Fuego. A Frenchman named Kerguelen discovered an island in 50° 5' S. lat., and named it after himself. Cook named it Desolation-Island. In Cook's second voyage, 1772, he reached 67° 15' S. lat., and was stopped by ice. In 1774 he reached a spot 71° 10' S. lat., and 106° 54' W. long., and was again stopped by ice. He afterwards discovered New Georgia, on which he said "not a tree was to be seen, nor a shrub big enough to make a toothpick." This is in 54° 55' S. lat. He then discovered Sandwich Land, and declared that "no man would ever go South farther than he had gone." After this, the Terra Australis Incognita (unknown Southern Continent), which had been drawn on most published maps, was omitted by geographers.

To be Continued in our next.

PHONETICS VERSUS FOGYISM.

A writer in the *N. Y. Tribune* on the subject of adopting a phonetic dress for our literature says, "We object to it simply as a matter of taste. We like the present dress of the language because of the dear and hallowed associations which link it in every cultivated mind with all that is beautiful and holy in our literature. It is not with us a matter of reason, but one of feeling."

Of this feeling of attachment to old, familiar objects, even though inanimate and of little value, we confess to the possession of our full share. An old chair or an old book-case, even, is not readily relinquished for the new-fangled devices of modern fashion. But our fondest attachments of this description may with propriety give way to considerations of important utility. There was in our childhood's day a rural charm in surveying those large Pennsylvania wagons, of three tires and six horses, as they wended their way—westward, ho!—o'er hill and dale, with tinkling bells and measured tread, bearing the merchandise of eastern cities to the then 'far West' of Pittsburg and Erie and adjacent regions, to return with the products of the virgin soil; but few, it is likely, will regret the displacement of those cumbrous vehicles by the comparatively modern improvements of canals and railroads. And if in physical labors the slow and awkward gives place to the more expeditious and skillful, why not in the intellectual culture?

But whatever may be the weight of this argument of feeling against the change of orthography in our printing generally, it can certainly have little importance against the use of phonetic spelling as a medium through which to acquire the reading of our present literature, which is in fact the only point that phoneticians in general are disposed to urge. Against the former only does the writer above alluded to, allege the objection, while he advocates the latter. But I have chosen to present it thus fully, from the belief that an indefinite and undefined influence from the same source operates insensibly against the latter use of phonetics also; while the objection needs but to be mentioned to make its want of reason manifest. It is the unusual aspect of a page of phonetic type that renders it so forbidding to the unaccustomed reader. He tries a little to peruse, but with indifferent success, for he attaches no fixed sounds to the characters employed.

The old orthography has not taught or even permitted him to attach fixed sounds to letters; but to do so is the indispensable key of the new, and that without which one neither sees nor can see any of its scientific accuracy or beautiful simplicity. He reads it as uncouthly as the blacksmith would apply to the instruments of watchmaking. He probably throws down the page in disgust, wholly blind to the beauties or the uses of which phoneticians speak. He concludes that the ways of our fathers are ways of wisdom still on this subject. Such will not deny in the general that the world is advancing; but are ready to remonstrate if it tends to move in a path which they have not marked out. But it has moved heretofore, and it did not always move in the way people thought it would. Who expected forty years ago to ride through the country on iron rails at the rate of five or six hundred miles a day? or to transact business a thousand miles distant through the medium of a simple wire? But these things are acknowledged facts; and certain other facts, facts in educational progress, are not less true or important, though less apparent to common observation. When the writer received his first introduction to geography in a very respectable academy in the State of New York, a volume of about 400 pages was placed in his hands, of as dry statistics, interspersed with nearly as dry description, as ever graced a United States census—and this too without map or chart or any visible illustration; nor is it known that a single map was at that time in the institution. And what a contrast between this mode of acquiring geographical knowledge and the facilities which are now furnished, as, for example, in the use of "Camp's Geography" and "Mitchell's Outline Maps!" And who can calculate the increase of this kind of knowledge, with all its attendant advantages, which has resulted from the change? A child will acquire more useful information on the subject now in a month than could then be obtained in a year; and those conversant with education for forty years, can discern equally advantageous changes in other departments of instruction, not to speak of such entire departments as have sprung into existence in that time.

But here I must ask a simple question of the reader: Were those teachers who thought maps unnecessary then, and who would not trouble themselves to learn how to use them, who preferred rather to hear the child repeat the words of the book without illustration—I ask, Were such teachers old fogies, or not? or were they advancing the best interests of education? If they were mistaken in their procedure then, are those who think they have reached the ultimatum of improvement now quite sure to be right? Though they have mastered the curriculum of to-day, and see nothing beyond, is it any more certain that improved modes of instruction have ceased to be possible than it was then? Corresponding improvements have been made in some other departments, though not in all. The mode of teaching to read has remained essentially unchanged. Here and there some slight advantage has been gained over the old A, B, C practice, in the adoption of SWAN's or WRIGHT's method, either of which succeeds for a few lessons, if skillfully used, but has not within itself the means of surmounting the chief difficulty. It leaves the enormous load of orthographic anomalies to rest upon sheer memory still; and neither of these methods has attained more than a very limited use. The vast majority of children are taught in the old way—of learning first to call the letters by their old and, in part, very uncouth names; and then, in combining them, to receive the pronunciation of each word direct from the teacher's mouth. The first part of the process facilitates learning to read as much as a journey to Long's Peak would the object of reaching New York; and the second part remains to constitute the herculean labor of 'one of the most difficult of human attainments', which no expedients like the above named methods have ever been able materially to diminish. But the judicious use of phonetics *will* accomplish this end; will enable the learner to master our present orthography with a greatly diminished amount of labor. To this conviction every intelligent and unprejudiced investigator of the subject has invariably come. We have never heard of an exception, nor do we expect to hear of one, any sooner than we hear of a disbeliever in the laws of gravitation. It is on this account, and for the other great advantages that such a mode of teaching will bring with it, that we especially desire the teachers of Illinois to look into the matter. Why should we keep our children traveling over that long, tedious road of misty bewilderment, when a comparatively short, plain and well-illuminated path is easily accessible? If it is from the fear of something new and a love of the good old ways of our fathers, then let us pursue a like course with geography, and throw away all our maps and globes and modern text-books, and set our classes to commit to memory, without explanation, whole volumes of matter like the following: "Massachusetts is 150 miles long and 60 broad. It is between 41° 30′ and 43° N. Lat., and between 69° and 73° W. Long. It is divided into the following counties" (giving their names), etc., etc., etc. But if we are not prepared to take old things in general, why hold on to a few which are no better than others that have been rejected? Why not examine all things and hold fast that which is good?

But permit me to say to any one who would examine this subject, do not pass judgment without a personal knowledge of the elementary sounds of our language. This knowledge, this indispensable requisite to a correct judgment, is lamentably wanting even among teachers, though none can teach correct pronunciation without it. Not long ago I heard a popular instructor express surprise at the declaration that the names of the letters and their sounds did not coincide. Of what value would be the judgment of such men on the use of phonetic instruction? Just as much as that of blind men on the merits of a landscape-painting, and no more; neither understands what he says, nor whereof he affirms.—*Ill. Teacher.*

PHILANTHROPY, was said by that reverend joker, Sidney Smith, to be the universal sentiment of the human heart, for whenever A. sees B. in trouble, he always wants C. to relieve him.

NEVER dispute about trifles, even though you are certain of being in the right. The truth will come to light sooner or later, and then your opponent will not only respect your wisdom, but love your meekness.

MOST MARVELLOUS CONJURING.

The Russians have long exhibited a remarkable taste for juggling and all that smacks of the marvellous. Conjurers, professors of natural magic, ventriloquists, and the entire race of mountebanks, who in France and England astonish the gaping crowds at races and country fairs, ever find a ready welcome and liberal encouragement among the higher classes in the Russian cities. About the beginning of the present century, a species of Cagliostro, or rather a superior kind of Wizard of the North, made his appearance at St. Petersburg, and astonished the natives by his marvellous performances. His name was Pirnetti, and his fame is yet retained in the memory of those who have witnessed his unrivalled talents.

The Czar Alexander, having heard Pirnetti much spoken of, was desirous of seeing him, and one day it was announced to the conjurer that he would have the honor of giving a representation of his magical powers at court, the hour fixed for him to make his appearance being seven o'clock. A brilliant and numerous assembly of ladies and courtiers, presided over by the Czar, had met, but the conjuror was absent. Surprised and displeased, the Czar pulled out his watch, which indicated five minutes after seven. Pirnetti had not only failed in being in waiting, but he had caused the court to wait, and Alexander was not more patient than Louis XIV. A quarter of an hour passed, half an hour, and no Pirnetti! Messengers, who had been sent in search of him, returned unsuccessful. The anger of the Czar, with difficulty restrained, displayed itself in threatening exclamations.

At length, after the lapse of an hour, the door of the saloon opened, and the gentleman of the chamber announced Pirnetti, who presented himself with a calm front and the serenity of one who had nothing to reproach himself with. The Czar, however, was greatly displeased; but Pirnetti assumed an air of astonishment, and replied with the greatest coolness, "Did not your Majesty command my presence at seven o'clock precisely?"

"Just so!" exclaimed the Czar, at the height of exasperation.

"Well, then," said Pirnetti, "let your Majesty deign to look at your watch and you will perceive that I am exact, and that it is just seven o'clock."

The Czar, pulling out his watch violently, in order to confound what he considered a downright piece of insolence, was completely amazed. The watch marked seven o'clock! He looked at the clock of the saloon, which had been twenty times consulted during the space that the assembly were kept waiting; the clock also marked and struck seven o'clock! In turn, the courtiers drew out their watches, which were found, as usual, exactly regulated by that of their sovereign. Seven o'clock! indicated with a common accord all the clocks and watches of the palace. The art of the magician was at once manifested in this strange retrogression of the march of time. To anger succeeded astonishment and admiration. Perceiving that the Czar smiled, Pirnetti thus addressed him: "Your Majesty will pardon me. It was by the performance of this trick that I was desirous of making my first appearance before you. But I know how precious truth is at court; it is really necessary that your watch should tell it to you, sir. If you will consult it now, you will find that it marks the real time."

The Czar once more drew forth his watch—it pointed to a few minutes past eight; the same ratification had taken place in all the watches of those present, and in the clocks of the palace. The exploit was followed by others equally amusing and surprising.

At the close of the performance, the Czar, after having complimented Pirnetti, brought back to his remembrance that, in the course of the evening's amusements, he had declared that he could penetrate everywhere.

"Yes, sire, everywhere," replied the conjurer, with modest assurance.

"What!" exclaimed the Czar, "could you penetrate even into this palace, were I to order all the doors to be closed and guarded?"

"Into this palace, sire, even into the apartment of your majesty, quite as easily as I should enter into my own house," said Pirnetti.

"Well, then," said the Czar, "at mid-day to-morrow I shall be ready in my closet with the price of this evening's amusement, one thousand roubles. Come and receive them. But I forwarn you that the doors shall be carefully closed and guarded."

"To-morrow at mid-day I shall have the honor of presenting myself before your majesty," and he bowed and withdrew.

Two gentlemen of the household followed the conjurer, to make sure he quitted the palace; they accompanied him to his lodgings, and a number of the police surrounded the dwelling from the moment he entered it. The palace was instantly closed, with positive orders not to suffer, under any pretext whatever, any one to enter, were he prince or valet, until the Czar himself should command the doors to be opened. These orders were strictly enforced—confidential persons having watched their execution. The exterior openings to the palace were guarded by the soldiery. All the approaches to the imperial apartments were protected by high dignitaries, whom a simple professor of the art of legerdemain possessed no means of bribin   In short, for greater security, all the keys had been carried into the imperi abinet. A few moments previous to the hour fixed for Pirnetti's interview with the Czar, the chamberlain on service brought to his majesty a dispatch wh ch a messenger had handed him through an opening in the door. It was a report from the minister of police that Pirnetti had not left home.

"Aha! he has found out that the undertaking is impracticable, and he has abandoned it," observed the Czar, with a smile.

Twelve o'clock sounded. While the last stroke yet reverberated, the door which communicated from the bedroom of the Czar to the cabinet opened, and Pirnetti appeared. The Czar drew back a couple of paces, his brow darkened, and after a momentary silence, while fixing a suspicious look on Pirnetti, he said, "Are you aware that you may become a very dangerous individual?"

"Yes, sire," he replied, "I am a humble conjurer, with no ambition but that of amusing your majesty."

"Here," said the Czar, "are a thousand roubles for last night, and a thousand more for this day's visit."

Pirnetti, in offering his thanks, was interrupted by the Czar, who with a thoughtful air inquired of him, "Do you count on yet remaining some time in St. Petersburg?"

"Sire," he replied, "I intend setting off this week, unless your majesty orders a prolongation of my sojourn."

"No," hastily observed the Czar, "it is not my intention to detain you; and moreover," he continued, with a smile, "I should vainly endeavor to keep you against your will. You know how to leave St. Petersburg as easily as you have found your way into this palace."

"I could do so, sire," said Pirnetti; "but, far from wishing to quit St. Petersburg stealthily or mysteriously, I am desirous of quitting it in the most public manner possible, by giving to the inhabitants of your capital a striking example of my magical powers."

Pirnetti could not leave like an ordinary mortal; it was necessary that he should crown his success in the Russian capital by something surpassing his previous efforts; therefore he announced that he should leave St. Petersburg the following day at ten o'clock in the morning, and that he should quit all the city gates at the same moment. Public curiosity was excited to the highest degree by this announcement. St. Petersburg at that time had fifteen gates, which were encompassed by a multitude eager to witness this marvellous departure.

The spectators at these various gates all declared that, at ten o'clock precisely, Pirnetti, whom they all perfectly recognized, passed through. "He walked at a slow pace, and with head erect, in order to be better seen," said they, and "he bade us adieu in a clear and audible voice." These unanimous testimonies were confirmed by the written declaration of the officers placed at every gate to examine the passports of travellers. The inspections of Pirnetti's passports were inscribed in the fifteen registers. Where is the wizard, whether coming from the north or south, who could perform so astonishing an exploit?

Ordinary "magicians" would feel rather nervous at the idea of undertaking the remarkable feats we have recited. We must remark, however, that, as regards the performance last mentioned, it does not appear to have been altogether original with Pirnetti. It is related of Cagliostro, that, receiving an order to leave Berlin, he went out in a coach-and-six through each of the six principal gates of the city at the same instant of time, exactly at 12 M. All the gate-keepers knew him, and testified to having seen him depart at that identical moment!

To Cato once a frightened Roman flew,—
The night before a rat had gnawed his shoe—
Terrible omen by the gods decreed :
"Cheer up, my friend," said Cato, "mind not that :
Though if, instead, your shoe had gnawed the rat,
It would have been a fearful sign indeed!"

QUESTIONS AND ANSWERS.

THE questions under this heading may be answered *in order* or not, as the reader prefers.

1. What is the proportion between the fall of rain in the tropics and that in the temperate zones?

ED.

2. When the elevation of the mercury in the barometer is 20 inches, what will be the height of a column of water supported by the atmosphere?

A. M.

3. Why will not writing paper absorb ink?

STUDENT.

4. What is the whole estimated quantity of rain on the surface of the earth?

IB.

Ans. In the Torrid zone the mean annual fall is $8\frac{1}{2}$ ft.; in the Temperate zones, $2\frac{1}{5}$ ft.; in the Frigid, $1\frac{1}{4}$ ft.: Total $12\frac{4}{5}$ ft.

ALLEN.

5. How are the tails of comets usually curved—and what is the cause of this curvature?

ED.

6. Why was the seat of government changed from Philadelphia to Washington?

ED.

7. A merchant gains annually 50 per cent. on his capital, of which he spends $300 per annum, and at the end of 4 years finds himself possessed of a sum 4 times as great as that with which he commenced business; what was his capital?

ED.

8. How old was Adam when Methusaleh was born?

ANNIE.

9. Where was the first locomotive used in the United States? (We should like to have this query answered.—ED.)

B.

10. Why are the bones of our arms, legs, &c., made hollow?

DR.

11. How is it that the sea is warmer in winter and cooler in summer than the land?

MID.

12. What part of 2 is 5? Required an explanation.

X.

13. Mention five words introduced into the English language within the past two centuries.

QUI.

14. Which prefix never changes its sound?

ALLA.

15. Why is it, that multiplying a number by 2, and dividing the product by 25, is the same as pointing off two decimal places in the multiplicand and multiplying by 8?

ED.

EDITORIAL MISCELLANY.

[THE Editor must apologize for the lack of original matter in this (and the last) number. In the March Number much space was taken up with an Extract from the Report of our worthy Superintendent of Public Schools, which we considered more acceptable than anything *we* could write—and at the very time when we should be in our *sanctum*, we are called to visit an Institute in a neighboring county.]

THE Conflagration of the William and Mary College at Williamsburgh, Va., a few weeks since, was a sad catastrophe. It was the oldest, except Harvard University, in the United States; it was chartered in 1692 by King William III and Queen Mary, who gave out of their private means nearly £2000 towards erecting the necessary buildings. This, with twenty thousand acres of land, and one penny a pound on all tobacco exported from Virginia and Maryland, granted in the charter, £2500 raised by subscription in the colony, and a gift of £200 from the House of Burgesses, constituted the endowment of the college. Within the last few years large additions have been made to the philosophical and chemical apparatus, both of which were amply sufficient for all the purposes of instruction in these sciences. The library has also been enlarged, and contained nearly 5000 volumes, among which are many curious and rare books.

ENGLISH Grammar has been defined as "the art of speaking and writing the English language correctly;" and this definition has been accepted and retained by grammarians, notwithstanding it has become a matter of public notoriety that pupils may excel in grammar and "parsing," as taught in our schools, and yet be unable to form grammatical sentences, either orally or in writing.

Where then, is the fault?—in the definition, or in the method of teaching? In the latter, we fully believe. The very fact that it is an art shows the absurdity of supposing that it can be acquired without practice. Who ever became a skillful musician simply by studying the principles and rules of music? Which of our great painters has become such but by intelligent, systematic and long-continued practice? The absurdity of determining never to go into the water till one has learned to swim, strikes us at once. Why not the equal absurdity of expecting to learn to write correctly without ever putting pen to paper? In the belief that the art of writing the language correctly can be obtained only by judicious, systematic and persevering practice, this book has been prepared. When the principles of grammatical construction have been applied until the habit is formed and we write correctly without reference to the rule, we then, and not till then, experience the beneficial results of the study of grammar. In the preparation of this book, our object has been, not to be profound, but practical. The fact that so many grammatical errors are found in the writings of the young and of those even, who are no longer young, will, we hope, be sufficient apology for the somewhat extreme exercises in grammatical forms. They are intended as a practical application of principles which have been learned in grammar, and which can be fully appreciated and fixed in the mind only by writing. The habit of writing grammatically being established, the next difficulty is in the argument. The pupil has facts enough at command, but how shall he begin, and by what method proceed? This difficulty we have attempted to remedy, and at the same time, so to simplify the work, that the attention of the pupil may be given to but one process at a time. If we have succeeded in this attempt, we believe that every teacher who has been in the habit of correcting the "compositions" of his pupils will admit that we have accomplished something well worth the labor.

With these designs, and with the hope and belief that we have done something to make the school exercise of writing composition less distasteful and more useful to the young, we commend this book to the examination of teachers and friends of education generally.—*Pref. of Tower's Gram. of Composition.*

THE population of Mormons in the United States and British dominions, in 1856, was not less than 68,700, of which 38,000 were resident in Utah; 5000 in New York State; 4000 in California; 5000 in Nova Scotia and the Canadas, and 9000 in South America. In Europe there were 39,000, of which 32,000 were in Great Britan and Ireland; 5000 in Scandinavia; 1000 in Germany; in Australia and Polynesia 2400; in Africa 100; and on travel, 2800. To these, if we add the different schismatic branches, including Strangites, Rigdonites and Wightites, the whole sect was not less than 126,000. In 1857, there appears to have been a decrease in the population of Utah—the number being only 31,022, of which 9000 were children, and about 11,000 men capable of bearing arms.

OUR NORMAL SCHOOL.—We stepped in for an hour or two to witness the examinations that were making in our Normal School during the past week, and we confess to have been highly delighted. The afternoon we were present, was devoted to Reading, Mental Arithmetic, Geography and Map drawing. All we saw and heard convinced us that the teaching was very thorough. Dr. Harvey has charge of the elocution, and his pupils read exceedingly well. There is no attempt at display, but natural and easy reading is what is sought after and very successfully obtained. In mental arithmetic, we made up our mind if all the editors of West Chester were put into one, they could not have answered a single one of the difficult questions propounded. It is the most severe mental discipline we have ever witnessed, and the class performed their duties with the highest credit. In map drawing the pupils display great facility and taste. The outlines of a country are placed upon the black-board with entire correctness, and the mountains, rivers, &c., are laid down with the precision of the engraved map. Prof. Allen, who is the laborious and faithful Principal of this growing and prosperous school, deserves great credit for the successful manner in which he has developed his pupils, and we hope the people of the county and elsewhere will remember that his school is deserving of their warmest encouragement.— *Village Record, Chester Co. Pa.*

NAMES OF WOMEN AND THEIR MEANING.—Mary, the commonest of all female names, is also one of the sweetest given to woman. It is not strange that it prevails so universally. Maria and Marie—the latter French, are only other forms of Mary, and, of course have the same meaning. Martha signifies bitterness; Anne, Anna and Hannah, and probably Nancy, are from the same source, and signify kind or gracious. Ellen was originally Helen—Helena in Latin, and Helene in French; according to some etymologists it has the meaning of alluring, but others define it as one who pities; Jane, now generally familiarized into Jenny, signifies like Anne, kind or gracious. For Sarah or Sally, there are two definitions—a princess, and the morning star. Susan signifies a lily, and is a fitting name for a tall, slender, flower-like girl, of delicate complexion and native grace. Rebecca, plump.—Lucy signifies like light, and was anciently given to girls born at daybreak. It may also be considered as meaning brightness of aspect, and applied accordingly. Bertha bright and Alberte, all bright. Louisa—in French, Louise—is the feminine of Louis, and signified one who protects. Fanny or Frances, means frank or free. Catharine, or Katherine, pure or chaste, is one of the best of our female names. Sophia from the Greek, means wisdom; Caroline and Charlotte, queens; Emma, tender, affectionate, motherly; Margaret, a pearl or a dalay; Julia, soft haired; Juliet and Julietta are the same as Julia; Agnes means chaste; Amelia, and Amy or Amie, beloved; Clara clear or bright; Eleanor all fruitful; Gertrude, all truth; Grace, favor; Laura, a laurel; Matilda, noble or brave maid; Phebe, light of life.

HAVE you seen the last edition of Mitchell's Atlas, published by E. H. BUTLER? You should get a copy and then go to Philadelphia and request Herr Kramer to show you the operations of Map-drawing, engraving, coloring, printing and binding.

SONGS WITHOUT WORDS.—BY CHARLES MACKAY.

Songs without words!—through forest leaves they quiver,
    With softer cadence tune the torrent's roar;
They mingle whispers with the rippling river,
    And sport in billows on the stormy shore.

Songs without words!—how often have I sung them
    In the fresh noon-time of my life's young day,
When hopes were free as if kind Heaven had flung them
    Plenteous as daisies in the lap of May.

Songs without words!—how often lonely musing,
    Fanned by the breath of morn, or evening skies,
Have joy and sorrow mutely interfusing,
    Throbbed in my veins and sparkled in my eyes.

Songs without words!—how oft in love's pure gladness,
    Her hand in mine, we've looked sweet songs unsung,
Of deeper joy and more entrancing sadness
    Than e'er found accents on a mortal tongue.   HOME JOURNAL.

GEORGE of Capadocia, born at Epiphania, in Cicilia, was a low parasite, who got a lucrative contract to supply the army with bacon. A rogue and informer, he got rich, and had to run from justice. He embraced Arianism, collected a library, and got promoted by faction, to the Episcopal throne of Alexandria. When Julian came, A. D. 361, George was thrown into prison, the prison was burst open by the mob, and George was lynched, as he deserved. And the precious knave became in good time the St. George of England, patron of chivalry, and the pride of the best blood of the modern world. Strange that the solid, truth-speaking Briton should derive from an imposter. Strange that the New World should have no better luck—that broad America must wear the name of a thief. Americo Vespuci, the pickle-dealer at Seville, who went out in 1499, a subaltern with Hojeda, and whose highest naval rank was boatswain's mate in an expedition that never sailed, managed in this lying world to supplant Columbus, and baptize half the world with his own dishonest name. Thus nobody can throw stones. We are equally bad off in our founders, and the false pickle-dealer is an offset to the false bacon-dealer.—*Emerson's English Traits.*

H. Cowperthwait & Co., 609 Chestnut str., Philadelphia, are the publishers of "Warren's Physical, Common School and Primary Geographies." They also publish "Greene's Series of English Grammars" and "Potter's Writing Books."

Clubbing with the Atlantic Monthly.—Our readers are informed that we can furnish the *Teacher's Journal* and the now celebrated *Atlantic Monthly* at the low price of $3.00 per annum. The regular price of the Atlantic is $3—so by taking the two monthlies you can get them for the usual price of one. In the December number of the Monthly was begun a serial by Mrs. Stowe. The renowned Autocrat of the Breakfast Table has committed—matrimony, but his friend, the Professor has taken lodgings in the same house, and talks so much like the Autocrat that one would suppose them to be brothers.

Send us $2 (if you are a subscriber) and we shall see that you receive a copy of the Atlantic Monthly for one year.

Revolutionary Soldiers.—During the past year, 1858, eighteen Revolutionary soldiers have died, viz: David Chapman, Gideon Bentley, John Titus, William Matteson, Robert Gallup, Zachariah Greene and David Davis of New York; Zacheus Robinson and Abraham Rising, of Massachusetts; Wm. Turkey and Rev. John Sawyer, of Maine; Thomas Kerowiltin and Elisha Mason, of Connecticut; George Wells and Charles Garman, of Tennessee; James Bushnell, of Vermont; Henry Straight and John Frazer of Ohio. There are yet two hundred of the patriots of the Revolution living and receiving their pensions.

A great lie, says the poet Crabbe, 'is like a great fish on dry land; it may fret and fling, and make a frightful bother, but it cannot hurt you. You have but to keep still, and it will die of itself.'

Smith, Woodman & Co., 609 Chestnut str., Philadelphia. This firm is engaged in the publication of "Johnson's Philosophical Charts."

The late firm of Sheldon, Blakeman & Co., publishers of Stoddard's Arithmetics, Keetel's French Course, &c., &c., is changed to Sheldon & Co. They are to be found at 115 Nassau str., N. Y., as before.

An Effect of Good Reading.—A clergyman, a lawyer and a doctor were members of one of Prof. Bronson's classes in elocution, and when the question—What shall be our class-book? came up, the minister wished the Bible could be used; but he remained silent, as the lawyer was an infidel.

The lawyer said. "Let us take the Bible; for I never could see any meaning in it till lately, when I heard some verses read from it by a good reader. It there is any sense in it I want to find it." So the Bible was used by them as a class-book.

Accent, emphasis, inflections, pauses, etc., etc., were explained and illustrated by examples. Darkness was visible. Twilight came. Morning dawned; and things near were clearly distinguished. Then the sun came up; it was full day. How had these treasures, on the very surface of the text, been concealed by bad reading? As the class repeated the examples given, a mine of truth was opened to them—philosophy shone in every line. Hope sprang up and blossomed, and Faith fixed roots deep in the soul. As the reading was, from time to time resumed, the modulations of the voice developed significance, and Revelation shone in its own light—simple, mighty unto salvation.

The soul of the unbeliever was bowed; it cried, "Lord! I believe." What had been dark, was full of glory. What he had called trash, proved the "pearl of great price." What he thought folly, was profound wisdom. In early years, had he been taught to read correctly, he would not have gone astray, thirsting as over deserts, when clear springs gushed all about him, hidden by verdure and flowers, he had trodden down as figures in the sand. But he had associated the Scriptures with school-boy blunders and nonsense. Never hearing the Bible read naturally, he saw only "the letter which killeth." As read now, he felt its spirit; and it gave him life. He became a Christian minister, converted by correct reading of the Scriptures. Were clergymen, generally, good readers, there would be fewer infidels. Many, in giving the Scriptures from the pulpit, make it contribute to spiritual death. Correct reading of the Bible is a condition without which it can not exert its vitality on the heart. If ministers who mourn that their labors are vain, would learn to read well, their churches would be filled with believers. As they sow, they reap.

Have you a copy of Webster's "Dictionary?" Do not neglect to have one before your next term begins.

Sower & Barnes are at 37 N. 3rd str., Philadelphia. They publish Prof. Brooks' "Normal Mental Arithmetic." Give them a call and examine their catalogue.

The labyrinth in Egypt contained three hundred chambers and two hundred and fifty halls. Thebes, in Egypt, presents ruins twenty-seven miles round. Athens was twenty-five miles round, and contained three hundred and fifty thousand citizens, and four hundred thousand slaves. The temple of Delphos was so rich in donations that its was plundered of five hundred thousand dollars— and Nero carried away from it two hundred statues. The walls of Rome were thirteen miles round.

Exhibitions in Schools.—A memorial, signed by sixty-five Principals of Grammar Schools in New York city, has been presented to the Board of Education, showing the ill effects of the annual exhibition of the writing, drawing and needle work of pupils of those schools. These teachers say, it is no just test of progress made in the branches thus attended to, that it results in injustice to the pupils, and that it draws disproportionate attention to these branches of study. Also, it causes estrangement, bitter feelings, and ungenerous rivalry among the teachers as well as among pupils. The memorial is strong against this display, and the ceremonies attending it. Good, indeed. The practice must prove injurious, especially to children naturally endowed with large approbativeness and small benevolence. There are higher motives than competition, holier feelings than rivalry with which to influence children. Besides, the affections are a means of influence unequaled in potency; by these the teacher may sway the pupil according to his pleasure. None who are ignorant of this available power should be employed as teachers of children. The unexceptionable influence is the better. It is safe and sure. Use it, teacher!—*Life Illus.*

RUBBERS should be put off whenever the wearer enters the house, and be worn as little as possible, because they are air tight, and restrain the perspiration of the feet. The air cannot be excluded from them or any portion of the body for any length of time, without sensibly affecting the health. It is our opinion that no habit tends more to good health than clean feet, and clean dry stockings, so as to allow the free perspiration of the nether extremities.—*Scien. Amer.*

As WE have no room for the many excellent articles we read during the month, we can do no better than to draw the attention of our readers to the Book, Periodical or newspaper in which they may be found. We are in the habit of keeping a memorandum of pieces which have interested us, so that when we wish to read on a particular subject, we may know where to find it discussed. Among those which we have read, we regard the following as especially worthy of attention.

"Study the Minds of your Pupils."—*Conn. Com. Sch. Jour.*, Nov., 1858.

"Good Manners."—*How. Col. Mag.*, Dec., 1858.

"Geography."—*Ala. Ed. Jour.*, Feb., 1859.

"Emma Willard."—*Am. Jour. of Ed.*, March, 1859.

"The Asteroids."—*Mich. Jour. of Ed.*, March, 1859.

"Prizes."—*Ind. Jour. of Ed.*, March, 1859.

"School Architecture."—*Ill. Teacher*, Jan., 1859.

THE HOME JOURNAL FOR 1859.—This deservedly popular family newspaper is this week filled, as usual, with all good things. It is a literary sheet of good sense, wit, humor, pathos and sentiment.—*Day Book.*

We have not seen the Home Journal for a long time. We used to pay $2 per annum for it.—[ED.

IF you fail to receive your Journal regularly, let us know *at once.*

ALLOW us to call attention to the "Teachers' Advertising Page." We charge Teachers *nothing.* Persons advertising for teachers are charged at the rate of $2 for each insertion of not more than five lines.

WE are always glad to hear from Teachers. Write to us when you please. We can not always *answer* your letters, owing to press of other business—but will acknowledge the receipt of every epistle sent to us.

CHANGE IN SCHOOL LAW.—The following bill is now pending before the Legislature of Pennsylvania, which provides for some important changes in the school law. The first, third and fourth sections were adopted in the Senate a few days ago, and the second and fifth negatived, when the bill was postponed for the present. The principal object aimed at in the bill, is the abolition of the office of County Superintendent, which question will be submitted to a vote of the people.

SECTION 1. Be it enacted by the Senate and House of Representatives of the Commonwealth of Pennsylvania in General Assembly met, and it is hereby enacted by the authority of the same; That when the directors or controllers and teachers of the several school districts in this Commonwealth shall have made the selection of books provided for in the twenty-fifth section of an act for the regulation and continuance of a system of education by common schools, approved the eighth day of May, one thousand eight hundred and forty-four, the books so selected shall be used for a period of not less than three years, and no change or alteration shall be made within that period.

SEC. 2. That it shall not be lawful, after the passage of this act, for the directors or controllers of common schools or any school district in this Commonwealth, to employ any female as teacher in the common schools, who has not attained the age of eighteen years, and no male applicant under the age of twenty years.

SEC. 3 That before any director of common schools hereafter elected shall discharge any of the duties imposed upon him by existing laws, he shall be qualified by oath or affirmation, to be administered by an acting justice of the peace or alderman, to faithfully and impartially discharge the duties of his said office.

SEC. 4. That it shall not be lawful for the school directors or controllers of the common schools of any school district in this State, in determining the amount of tax to be levied in their district for school and building purposes, to exceed eight mills on the dollar on any and all property subject to taxation by existing laws for school purposes.

SEC. 5. That all independent school districts heretofore formed, either by enactment of the Legislature or by any court of common pleas of this Commonwealth, be and the same are hereby abolished : and that it, shall not be lawful for the said courts, after the passage of this act, to establish or continue any independent district for school purposes.

SEC. 6. That the qualified electors of the several cities, boroughs and counties of this Commonwealth shall, at the next general election, determine by ballot whether the office of county superintendent of common schools shall be abolished or not ; and that the ballots so voted shall be for the county superintendent and against the county superintendent ; and the result of said election shall be certified by the proper officers in the mode prescribed by existing laws in relation to the returns for State officers ; and if a majority of the votes polled should be against the abolition of said office, then the same shall remain as provided for by existing laws : but if a majority of the votes so polled should be in favor of the abolition of the office, then the said office is to be so declared abolished by the State Superintendent of common schools. to take effect on the first Monday in January next succeeding said election ; notice of the same to be sent by said State superintendent in the Commonwealth.

SEC. 7. That in case the people should decide in favor of the abolition of the office of County Superintendent as hereinbefore provided for, then it shall be the duty of the board of directors or controllers of common schools, of the several districts of this Commonwealth, to annually appoint three competent persons, who shall constitute a board of examiners, for the examination of applicants for employment as teachers. in conjunction with the aforesaid directors or controllers ; and no other persons, except such as shall be recommended by said examiners, shall be employed as teachers.

To the 1st section we heartily subscribe our hand and seal this bright April morning.

Number 2 we oppose. Many of our best female teachers are under eighteen —there are better ones developing in the schoolroom.

Number 3—Amen. Why not? his office is one of the most responsible within the gift of the people.

Numbers 6 and 7 we unhesitatingly oppose. Our reasons we may give at some future time.

PERISCOPE.

The Russian government has provided for the establishment of twenty Military Schools in which Surveying, Topographical Engraving, Gymnastics, &c., shall be taught to the sons of poor nobles gratuitously, on condition that they serve the state for a certain number of years.

The number of schoolhouses in Missouri is 3,380. She spends $180,000 this year for school purposes.

· In Indiana, they sell the school at auction to the *lowest bidder*, that is, to the man who engages to *keep* it (not teach) for the smallest amount of money per quarter!

Wisconsin pays $2 a year for the education of each child she sends to school.

Iowa—The School Law of this State has been declared unconstitutional.

Ohio employs 19,900 common school teachers, sends 356,000 children to school. pays her teachers $1,975,800, and has invested in school property $3,850,000.

Illinois—460,000 children attend school in this state—20,000 (according to Superintendent Powell's Report) patronize Private Schools. Number of schools 10,238. School term 6⅔ months.

Washington, D. C., contains 10,700 children old enough to attend school. 5,000 receive no education except in the street!

There are upwards of 3,000 coal mines in Great Britain, which employ nearly 250,000 men, women and boys. The working capital invested is estimated at £30,000,000, the annual 'get' of coal at 34,000,000 tons, and the value thereof at the pit's mouth is £10,000,000. Not one penny of this enormous income is expended for the education of these poor people, some of whom *see day-light* once in a lifetime!

North Carolina—The Superintendent of Common Schools reports the whole number of white children in the State to be 220,000. The number of schools from 3,700 to 3,800. The number of children attending school 155,000—an increase of 2,000 over last year's report. The number of children attending private schools, &c., 15,000. The superintendent asserts that "the proportion of wholly illiterate persons among the rising generation will be vastly less than among those whose places they will take; less, according to present appearances, than that among their contemporaries in a very considerable majority of the States of the Union." There are in the state, 1,994 male teachers and 205 female teachers who are reported as licensed. The average length of the school term for the past year, was 3⅖ months and the average salary of teachers, $23.62 per month.

Massachusetts—The number of public schools in this State in 1858, was 4421; Teachers 7184—male 1691, female 5493. The number of scholars in attendance during the summer was 198,702; during the winter, 218,198. The average pay of male teachers $49.87 per month, that of female teachers $19.63.

PERIODICALS, &c.

"Family and School Journal," published by Townsend & McCalla, Phila., a weekly Journal devoted to the interests of Literature, Education and Art. It is another specimen of the success of Young American effort. Price $2 a year.

"Doylestown Democrat,"—a first-rate country paper. Published at Doylestown, Bucks county, Pa. at $2 per annum. One of the best advertising papers in East Pennsylvania.

"Journal de L'instruction publique," Montreal (Bas-Canada—Lower Canada) Motto—"Religion, Science, Liberty, Progress, to make the people better;"—Good —and juding from present appearances, our French friends are doing their best to attain this last object. But *ami Journal*, as your *Corneille* says: *le ciel sur nos souhaits ne regle pal les choses.* Were it so, then would there be no need of our labor friend Journal. We hope however that you are receiving some recompense for your toil. Trust to Providence—but as Cromwell said to his men— keep your powder dry.

"Barnard's American Journal of Education." The number for March has been received. To praise this great Educational Journal were merely to repeat what the press all over country say of it. Read the articles on Mrs. Willard, Thos. H. Burrowes and Pestalozzi—either one is worth the price of the periodical. Published at Hartford, Conn., at $3 per annum.

"School Visitor," Spencerport, N. Y. A fine little eight-page paper, containing a variety of useful and amusing articles. It is published by the school-commissioner of Monroe county, N. Y., and is devoted to the interests of Common Schools. 50 cents per annum.

"Chester County Times." (Pa.) The educational column in this weekly paper contains as much practical reading matter as many periodicals of more pretentious growth. The editor is a practical teacher—Fordyce A. Allen—*perhaps* some of our Pennsylvania subscribers know him. As a useful county paper we know of none superior to it.

"Rhode Island Schoolmaster." The February number of this useful and entertaining Monthly is the second of the fifth volume. Mowry promises to improve his Journal. We should like to see him do it. How he can afford this monthly feast for one dollar we can not understand. We hear that the Schoolmaster has a larger circulation *without* than *within* its own state. While we are happy to hear that it circulates everywhere, we feel like asking the Rhode Island Teachers, or rather those who are not subscribers, "are you not ashamed of yourselves?"

"Illinois Teacher." Welcome to our sanctum. We like you. In the first place we liked the cut of your jib, and on turning your cover, we liked you better still. You have not put the best on the outside. We shall always welcome you.

North Carolina is celebrated for its immense pine forests, its turpentine, tar, pitch and gold, but never for the facilities it has offered to its people for receiving the benefits of an education. We are happy to see that the work is in progress. The "N. C. Journal of Education" is undoubtedly one of the very best Educational Journals in the country, and is laboring *earnestly* in the good cause. It is published at Greensboro, N. C. at two dollars per annum. W. D. Campbell, Ed.

"Indiana School Journal." This is truly a valuable Journal. It should not have been called the "Indiana" Journal, for its teachings apply as well to Louisana or to Maine. It is a national work, and deserves the support of Teachers all over the country. It is published by the State Teachers' Association. W. D. Henkle, Editor, Indianapolis.

"Michigan Journal of Education,"—Edited by Alex. A. Winchell, A. M., Professor of Natural History in the Michigan University, Ann Arbor. Ten years ago, who would have looked for a 32 page Educational Journal in Michigan? Every teaching Michigander whose name is not on Winchell's book is a Michi-*goose*.

"The Printer," Henry & Huntingdon, N. Y. A monthly newspaper devoted to the interests of the "Art preservative of all Arts!" Price $1 a year. A creditable specimen of printing, and generally contains useful articles on every subject of general interest. The March number contains a paper on *Punctuation* which is worthy of attention.

"Mathematical Monthly." Edited by J. D. Runkle, A. M., Cambridge, Mass., at $3 a year. It supplies a want long felt among Mathematicians. The March number contains some excellent articles. "The Order of Mathematical Studies" so extensively copied by Educational Journals, was written for the Monthly.

"The Boys' and Girls' Magazine." This interesting little monthly is published by Wm. L. Jones, 152 6th Avenue, New York, at 75 cents a year. It is a well conducted work, and is as instructive as many of larger growth.

"Merry's Museum." We well remember Robert Merry. We met him fifteen years ago when we were just beginning to read. We subscribed for Merry's Museum and have our bound volume still. Merry's Museum is published in New York $1 a year.

"Educational Herald and Musical Monthly." This periodical containing, each month, original and selected educational articles, besides information concerning Science, Art and Literature, is published by Smith & Woodman whose advertisement appears in the present number of the Journal. The Herald always contains something good.

"The New Hampshire Journal of Education" is published by the N. H. State Teachers' Association at $1 a year; Henry A. Sawyer, Resident Editor, Concord, New Hampshire. We have received but the April number and would thank the editor for the back numbers of this volume. We welcome this Journal to our table, confident, from what we have seen of its last number, that we shall never read it without learning something new—without being better able to discharge our duties as a teacher. It is a useful and instructive monthly, and we hope our Yankee friends in the Granite State will not allow it to droop for want of support.

OUR BOOK TABLE.

"THE Scholar's Companion," a hand-book of Etymology is published by E. H. BUTLER & Co., of Philadelphia. This work is from the pen of Rufus Bailey, who has devoted much attention to its preparation. The majority of words in daily use are traced to their sources—Latin, Greek, French, &c., &c., and are systematically arranged under their respective roots. Thus after reading the Latin or Greek root, the pupil is enabled to discover the relation between it and its English derivatives. We have known this book for a long time, but we have seldom known it to be rightly used. It can be made a most useful aid in the acquisition of the English language. It is the best school-book on Etymology extant.

G. S. HILLARD is the author, of a very attractive little primer called "The First Primary Reader." It is printed on tinted paper, which is more grateful and less injurious to the eye than that commonly used in books of this kind. The engravings by Billings and Andrews are the most beautiful we have ever seen in a school-book. The reading lessons are very simple—the words used are frequently repeated, and are thus more strongly impressed upon the memory. We are pleased to see this growing inclination to improve the appearance of Elementary text-books. This constant contact with the beautiful develops in the child a love of the beautiful.

"The First Primary Reader" is published by HICKLING, SWAN & BREWER, Boston.

"SPRAGUE's Natural Philosophy," PHILLIPS, SAMSON & Co., 13 Winter street, Boston. The want of a work of this kind has long been felt. This is not a mere *treatise*—it is a practical hand-book of Natural Philosophy, containing not only a statement of the laws of the material world, but instructions in the use of the apparatus which is required to illustrate those laws. Thousands of dollars have been expended for Philosophical Apparatus, the operating of which was not understood by those who attempted to use it. To those whose schoolrooms are supplied with apparatus (and we hope their numbers may soon increase) we cheerfully recommend the use of Sprague's Elements.

"RICORD's Roman History," A. S. BARNES & BURR, New York. To the already large list of Histories of Rome, is added another, whose claims upon the attention of Educators are great. It does not pretend to be a complete History of Rome, but presents, in a pleasing and attractive manner, the Legends and authentic narratives of Rome, from the building of the city B. C. 752 to its abandonment after the building of Constantinople A. D. 337. It is divided into three parts, the Monarchy, the Republic and the Empire. At the end of each of these divisions is prepared a series of questions on the chapters immediately preceding.

This is in *all* respects a most attractive work. It is useful in the schoolroom, an ornament to the parlor table—and will prove a valuable edition to the teacher's library.

FROM the same house we have received a copy of "Brooks' Manual of Devotion," a little work which was formerly published in Baltimore and which we noticed in a former number of the Journal. In reading the Preface, (which we had not done before) we met with the following expression : "it is to be regretted that hitherto in the educational systems of our country, there has been so little recognition of God and of the *sanctions which religion gives to morality and virtue.*" What does this mean? Has our friend reference to *all* the systems of education pursued in our country? It cannot be possible that he has ever visited the schools of his own city. (Baltimore.) Where shall we look for a system of education which shall recognize God and shall inculcate principles of morality and virtue, if not to our own Public School System? Every man, poor or rich, native or alien, has a right to educate his child in the Common School. The child is taught from his entrance into the school, that every American has a right to think as he pleases—he is taught that he is *one* among many who are to hold the reins of government when the fathers of the present generation have passed away —and he feels his responsibilty. In a great majority of the Common Schools of the country, the Bible is daily read—many of our text-books abound in selections and extracts from the Good Book—in short, we contend that the Public School System is the *source* of religion and virtue and morality among the mass of our people. Go to our large cities where the "Gospel (should be) preached to the *poor.*" What inducement is there given for the ignorant poor man to attend divine service? *He* perhaps has never been taught principles of virtue and morality—*he* does not feel at home in the house of God—his neighbor in broadcloth has his cushioned seat and his velvet-bound prayer book—*he* must occupy a hard bench in a remote part of the house—he is *not* on a social equality with the rich man. These remarks will not apply to *all* churches. Thank Heaven there are a few in which the poor man, though he knows that in his "Father's house there are many mansions" feels that there is one at least in which he and his more favored brothers may meet on terms of equality.

Go now to the Public School; there you find the sons of rich and poor on the same seat—in the same class—in the same game on the same playground. No false partition separates them—no unpleasant distinctions are made here. The Bible is heard by all alike—its precepts are applied to and by all alike. There is an equality here, which in Free America erases the degrading difference in worldly wealth from the mind—and leaves it free to receive the waters of truth unpolluted by the mud of jealousy and envy.

No, friend Brooks, if you allude to the Public School System of this country, in this sweeping assertion of yours, we deny it—and attribute your remark to a complete ignorance of the practical working of the system.

But the Preface of this little work will not diminish its worth as an Exercise-book. We are confident that it will be welcomed by many a teacher who heretofore has been obliged to confine himself to a dry routine of prayer making in order to meet the requirements of his community.

WANTS.

1 Wanted—A male Teacher for a school in Lehigh county, to teach the remainder of the term (2 months.) Apply by letter to the Editor of "Teacher's Journal."

2 Mr. ——— aged 23, a native of Pennsylvania, wishes a situation as teacher in a district school. (Mr. 3 has not sent us his certificate.)

3 Mr. ——— aged 30, a native of Pennsylvania, wishes a situation as teacher in a borough or district school. Certificate from Westmoreland county, grade 1½. Certificate from Montgomery county, grade 1½. Teaches English only.

4 Mr. ——— aged 25, a native of Philadelphia county, wishes a situation as teacher in a borough or township school. Graduate of the Philadelphia High School. Can teach Latin and Greek.

5 Mr. ——— aged 20, wishes a situation. No certificate.

6 Mr. ——— wants a situation as teacher; is competent to teach all the common English branches. References given if required.

[If we are called upon to give any particulars in regard to number 5 we must plead inability of course. He has not sent the copy of his certtficate, nor has he told us anything more than that he *wishes to teach*.]—ED.

☞THIS PAGE OF WANTS is offered by the Editor to those who are in want of Situations as Teachers. From *Teachers* we take NO PAY for our trouble. Those who advertise for Teachers are charged $2 for *five lines and less*. The money must in all cases accompany the notice.

As our facilities for becoming acquainted with Teachers and Directors and Communities are great, we shall take advantage of this fact to recommend the proper man for the proper place.

In answering these advertisements mention particularly the number of the Journal in which they appeared, and also the separate numbers appended to the advertisements.

All applications (except where the notice itself provides otherwise) are to be made by letter to   R. W. McALPINE, Ed. Teacher's Journal,

Allentown, Pa.